This Book Belongs To:

The Muppet Babies live in a nursery
in a house on a street that is a lot like yours.
But they can travel anywhere anytime using a special power—
the power of the imagination.
Can you imagine what it would be like to go with them?
Join the Muppet Babies on this adventure and find out.

Weekly Reader Presents

Baby Piggy and the Giant Bubble

By Dina Anastasio • Illustrated by Tom Cooke

Muppet Press/Marvel

J
A

Piggy's adventure began about eight,
When most of the Babies had sat down to wait
For Nanny to bring them their cereal bowls,
Their glasses of juice, and their cinnamon rolls.

In a bowl, Piggy mixed up some soap and some water,
Then dipped in her pipe, just like Nanny had taught her,
And blew out some bubbles, all shiny and bright,
That floated and glittered, reflecting the light.

Piggy watched one big bubble sail up to the ceiling.
She closed her eyes tight and imagined the feeling
Of drifting and soaring up into the air,
Inside of that bubble to heaven knows where.

And she suddenly was! She was floating up high,
Out the nursery window and into the sky!

She bounced toward a tree and then came down to rest
In a newly-made, slightly staid, tidy, trim nest
Filled with tiny blue eggs less than half Piggy's size.
"Blue eggs!" Piggy said. "What a pleasant surprise!"

Just then, in a rush, a plump robin flew by.
She stopped and she stared, then she let out a cry.
For one of her eggs was unusually big,
And what's more, that big egg held a cute little pig.

The mother bird squawked. The mother bird fluttered.
She leaned very close to the bubble and muttered,
"A pig in my nest! Why that doesn't seem right.
I hope you won't mind if I seem impolite.
You're a bit out of place, so you really can't stay."
Then, with one gentle push, she sent Piggy away.

A breeze caught the bubble. Away Piggy went,
Till she blew through the door of a big circus tent.

As the audience clapped, Piggy bounced off the knees
Of an upside-down man on a flying trapeze,
Who gave her a kick, and she landed intact
Smack-dab in the midst of a juggler's act.

The juggler just flipped. There'd been nine balls and now
There were ten in the air, and he didn't know how
To juggle that many. "Oh, dear," Piggy said,
As he fumbled the balls and they fell on his head.

Piggy was juggled right out of the tent.
She circled a street light, then made a descent
Near a stadium filled with a crowd watching soccer.
"What's that?" yelled a soccer fan. "Somebody block her!"

But no one could stop her. She just missed the mayor,
Then bounced off the toe of a shocked soccer player.
The bubble spun out and careened round a pole.
Then it whizzed past the stands to the other team's goal.

"Goal!" called the ref, and the winning team cheered.
"I protest!" cried the kicker. "A pig interfered!"
"Pardon moi," Piggy said. "I don't mean to cause trouble.
I'm a pig, not a ball, just a pig in a bubble."

The ref tossed the bubble so far that it flew
Past the bus stop, the toy store, the park, and the zoo.

Then it blew through the smoke of a puffing freight train,
And the smoke puffed the bubble right up to a plane.

The pilot was spelling out words in the sky.
He didn't look up as the bubble flew by.
But when he was finished, he noticed an O
That didn't belong at the end of his GO.

"My GO!" gasped the pilot. "This never will do!
A GO with two O's isn't GO, it's just GOO!"

The bubble swooped down, looped around, and just then,
Piggy saw she was back near the nursery again.

The bubble stopped short near the top of a tree,
Where it came face to face with a striped bumblebee.

The bee eyed the bubble, and poor Piggy trembled.
She called to her friends, who all quickly assembled.
"Help!" Piggy shouted. "I think I'm in trouble.
One sting from this bee means the end of my bubble."

"We'll find a solution," called Kermit. "Don't worry."
"The sooner, the better!" said Piggy. "Please hurry."
After much consultation, involving debate,
They came up with a plan that was truly first-rate!
"We've got it!" cried Kermit. "We know what to do.
We'll send up a staircase of bubbles to you!"

The bee hovered closer. The bubble went "POP!"
Piggy bounced down the staircase and came to a stop
Right next to her friends on the nursery floor,
Just where she had left them a short time before.

Now travel is fun, and it stretches the mind.
It's great to explore all the places you find.
But when the trip ends, when you'd rather not roam,
You can take it from Piggy—there's no place like home!